8 50

AUKELE
THE FEARLESS

illustrated by Earl Thollander

Golden Gate Junior Books / San Carlos, California

AUKELE
THE FEARLESS

A legend of old Hawaii
by Vivian L. Thompson

To Rocky, Pieper, and Barney Toyama—
three brothers who made wiser use of their talents
than Aukele's brothers

Contents

Foreword

THE TALE OF AUKELE is thought to be one of Hawaii's oldest folk tales, originating in Tahiti and brought to Hawaii by its earliest settlers. It recounts the adventures of a young chief who sails for an unknown land, undertakes a perilous quest, overcomes formidable opponents, and wins a sorceress wife.

This type of tale is found in the folklore of many lands, but certain features of Aukele are uniquely Polynesian. The image of the god Lono who warns him of approaching danger. The feather shoulder cape which protects him from fire and reduces his enemies to ashes. The Water of Life he seeks to restore his lost brothers and nephew. The mo-o grandmother who provides magic talismans for his quest.

This mo-o figure, a kind of giant lizard, is found again and again in Hawaiian folk tales. A giant lizard in Hawaii? Where the most terrifying specimen is the harmless gecko who chirrups from the eaves after nightfall, scuttles along the walls in search of insects—a creature barely three inches long? Some scholars believe the dragon lizard may be a memory from very distant ancestors who once lived in an area terrorized by crocodiles. An interesting possibility.

So come adventuring with Aukele. Aukele who was carried off by his mo-o grandmother. Aukele who learned to fly and visited Thunder God and Moon God. Aukele who slew Halulu-the-evil-one and won a sorceress wife. Aukele the traveler. Aukele the fearless.

VIVIAN L. THOMPSON

Paauilo, Hawaii
September, 1971

AUKELE
THE FEARLESS

Ten Brothers–and Trouble

AUKELE WAS THE ELEVENTH son of High Chief Iku of Land-supporting-the-heavens. Not one of his ten sons had Iku ever held in his arms nor shown any affection. But Aukele, son of his old age, Iku cherished and promised him his chiefdom.

This favoritism earned for Aukele his brothers' resentment and dislike. Only his brother Iku-lani, nearest to him in age, felt any fondness for Aukele. Seeing this, the other brothers kept the two apart. Kama-kahi, the eldest brother, who should by custom have been his father's heir, looked on Aukele with a fierce hatred as having cost him his inheritance.

Kama-kahi ruled his brothers harshly, and because of his savage cruelty and quick temper, they dared not disobey him. He established a rigid schedule and trained them in pairs, each in one of the deadly arts of combat, until they became experts: two as boxers, two as wrestlers, two as spearsmen, two with the war club. Two—he and the next eldest brother—became bone-breakers, those dreaded fighters able to crack a man's arm or leg, to lift him high and snap his spine.

Aukele, eager to be accepted, worked diligently to earn a place with his brothers, but Kama-kahi ignored him. He took all but Aukele on a championship tour of the islands —a tour which had lasted nearly a year.

Yesterday, from the pali, Aukele had seen them return, flushed with success. Had run to greet them and been brushed aside. Had heard tall tales of their engagements with the Strong Man of Kauai, the Three Warriors of Oahu, the Spearsman King of Maui.

Today, from the same pali, Aukele looked down on the brothers relaxing in a friendly game of darts. He longed to be with them, but he did not blame them for their rejection. He was a youth now, tall and well-developed, but they still thought of him as their young tag-along brother. How could they know that he had spent the year of their absence in developing his strength and skill so that he might qualify for their company? How could they know . . . unless he brought the matter to their attention?

He went to a great boulder that lay nearby, lifted it easily, disclosing his secret hiding place. From it he took a dart made from the stem of a sugar cane tassel, tipped with clay in his own distinctive fashion. He carried it to the edge of the pali overlooking the playing field, waited until his eldest brother Kama-kahi had thrown his dart, then threw his.

It sailed down gracefully, skimmed along the field, and came to rest a good four feet beyond Kama-kahi's dart.

His eldest brother looked up, scowling, and barked an order to his brothers. Two of them, the expert boxers, started up the trail toward Aukele. He waited, smiling.

They reached the top of the cliff and came toward him. "Have you not learned to stay out of your brothers' games?" demanded the first. "Then we have come to teach you," said the second. They advanced confidently, one from the left, one from the right.

The first brother attacked, aiming a wicked blow to Aukele's chin. How was it then, that he found himself gathered up in Aukele's strong young arms and tossed with a resounding splash into the sea below?

The second brother came at him with an angry roar, aiming a murderous blow to Aukele's body. How was it then, that he found himself flying through the air and splashing into the sea behind his brother?

When the two returned, dripping, to Kama-kahi, he sent the two wrestling brothers to do what the boxing brothers had failed to do.

Aukele greeted them with a smile. "Do you seek your boxing brothers?" he asked. "Let me help you find them." Before either brother could get a firm hold, Aukele had gathered them up, one after the other, and tossed them into the sea after their brothers.

Before long, eight brothers had returned from a visit to Aukele, returned shamefaced and dripping sea water. Then Kama-kahi, filled with wrath, summoned his partner in bone-breaking and went up to meet Aukele face to face.

"You!" he roared. "Have you no respect for your elder brothers? Must we crack you in two before you learn?"

"Auwe, my brother, I am slow to learn," Aukele admitted. "But it will be an honor to be taught by my eldest brothers."

Kama-kahi's partner rushed at Aukele, planning to break his arm. Rushed at him and found himself flying through the air and splashing into the sea like his brothers before him.

Seeing this, Kama-kahi rushed at Aukele, planning to break both his arms. Rushed at him—and found himself flying through the air, landing in the sea with a humiliating splash before all his younger brothers.

The others shambled off, carefully avoiding any further contact with their youngest brother. But Kama-kahi stalked, dripping, from the sea, climbed the pali again, and returned to face Aukele. He held out his hand with a rueful grimace.

Aukele eyed it warily.

Kama-kahi looked at him with a wry grin. "You have reason to be suspicious," he conceded. "But you have made surprising progress during our absence and deserve now to be one of us. It is not right for brothers to quarrel so. Come home and share a meal with me and my young son, Sacred One."

Aukele's face glowed. His dream was coming true at last; Kami-kahi was accepting him. "Gladly," he answered.

On entering the men's eating house, Kama-kahi went directly to a great stone set in the center of the floor. "Your pardon, my brother," he said. "Before we eat I must provide food for my aumakua, who comes on the rising tide. Perhaps you would help me?" He indicated the heavy stone to be lifted.

Eagerly Aukele went to his assistance. As the stone lifted, he saw beneath it a yawning black pit. Before he could step back, Kama-kahi dealt him a stunning blow that sent him hurtling into the pit, down ... down ... down ... into inky darkness.

From above came the eerie sound of Kama-kahi's mocking voice, echoing through the black passage. Kama-kahi's voice crying, "Great Mo-o Woman, here is your food!"

HIGH CHIEF IKU

Great Mo-o Woman

WHEN AUKELE REGAINED CONSCIOUSNESS, he thought himself blind. Not a glimmer of light broke through the inky blackness of the pit. He struggled to his feet, relieved to find no bones broken. Stumbling, hands outstretched, he tried to locate a wall. Nothing met his groping hands. No sound broke the stillness except the distant rise and fall of the sea.

Then faintly, above the pounding of the surf, another sound reached him. Not from the sea but from overhead— from the mouth of the pit in Kama-kahi's home.

Someone was calling his name. Not Kama-kahi—a gentler voice than his—the voice of his young brother Iku-lani. It came again. "Au . . . ke . . . le?" The sound drifted down eerily. "Can . . . you . . . hear . . . me?"

"Ae, Iku. I can! Speak!" Aukele called.

"Listen carefully . . . Great Mo-o Woman is your grandmother! Tell her this! Perhaps she will spare you."

14

"Thank you, Iku-la—" Aukele broke off. He had heard a change in the sound of the sea. The tide was turning—and Kama-kahi had said Great Mo-o Woman came with the rising tide! Aukele, straining to hear, made out a splashing sound that drew nearer and nearer; heard the slithering sound of a monstrous body coming along the passage from the sea. Closer . . . closer . . . until Aukele felt a blast of hot breath as something out of the inky blackness picked him up, then swung about, and started back toward the sea.

"Wait, Great Mo-o Woman!" Aukele cried. But his cries were drowned by the increasing sound of crashing surf. At the end of the tunnel he caught a glimpse of light. It grew brighter as the lumbering creature carried him on, into a rocky cave overlooking the sea. Here, Great Mo-o Woman settled down to make a meal of him.

"Wait, Great Mo-o Woman!" Aukele cried again. "I am your grandson!"

The great jaws opened and Aukele fell with a thud to the rocky floor. Looking up, he had his first sight of his captor—a huge scaly body with tapering tail at one end, woman's head at the other. But what a head! A great gaping mouth with sharp, pointed teeth, heavy-lidded eyes, a shock of gray, matted hair.

"Is this a trick?" Great Mo-o Woman demanded, and the walls shook with the sound of her voice.

"No trick," Aukele assured her. "I am Aukele, last son of Iku and Kapapa, grandson of Chief-of-utter-darkness; your grandson, Mo-o Woman."

"How came you here?"

"My brother Kama-kahi threw me into the pit."

The great head nodded grimly. "That one!" exclaimed

15

Mo-o Woman with scorn. "Him I could eat with pleasure, but not you, my youngest grandson. Come! You and I will teach Kama-kahi a lesson. Your brothers plan to set out in search of an island. They will find two. The first, Holani-of-the-rising-sun, is small and beautiful; rich in sugar cane, bananas, coconut, and breadfruit; flowing with clear streams. Its people share these things happily. But will Kama-kahi be content there? He will not. He will seek a larger, more impressive island. And he will find it. Holani-of-the-setting-sun. It too is beautiful, with mountains to touch the stars. It too is rich in food plants and pure water. Yet those who live there are close to starvation."

"But why, Grandmother?"

Great Mo-o Woman snorted. "Because all are slaves—slaves of the Chiefess Namaka, who starves them. Slaves—just as your brothers will be—if they live."

"But we must save them!" Aukele cried. "You are powerful! You must know a way!"

The heavy-lidded eyes opened wider. "You would save them after they have treated you so?"

"No matter. They are my brothers," Aukele answered. "And young Iku—he is not like the others."

"True. He is not. Very well, Aukele. I will give you the power to save them—if they follow your advice! But if they ignore it, they will die. Bring me that calabash!"

On a shelf of the cave wall, Aukele saw a covered calabash. He went to the shelf and lifted it down carefully.

"Take out what you find inside," Mo-o Woman directed. Aukele did so. There were four objects: a small wooden image, a green leaf, a feather shoulder cape, a gleaming knife.

"These are my magic talismans," Great Mo-o Woman

16

explained. "The image is your family god, Lono. He will warn you of danger, tell you how to meet it. The life-giving leaf will satisfy your hunger and thirst. The feather cape, when worn, will protect you from fire, reduce your enemy to ashes when shaken. The knife is a magic one. You will know how to use it when the time comes."

Carefully Aukele replaced the talismans in the calabash and covered it again. "Thank you, my grandmother," he said. "Can you tell me more of this Chiefess Namaka?"

Great Mo-o Woman nodded. "She is a sorceress, very powerful and very well guarded. By two kupua maid servants who can take on rat and lizard forms. By four kupua brothers who can take on bird form. By a vicious dog, Moela, and an evil bird, Halulu. One thing you must remember—approach her peacefully! Otherwise you will never live to use my magic talismans."

"I understand, Grandmother," Aukele replied.

"Now I will lift you out," said Mo-o Woman. "Find your brothers and persuade them to take you with them. Unless they do, all of them will die."

The great head lowered, the great jaws opened. Aukele felt himself being lifted and carried out to the pali's edge. Far below, the surf crashed and broke upon a rocky shore. If Mo-o Woman let go now it would be the end of him. But she reached down and set him on a narrow path cut into the pali's face. Being careful not to look down from the dizzying height, Aukele, with the calabash under his arm, made his careful way up the trail. In the distance he could see his home and the home of Kama-kahi. He waved to Great Mo-o Woman, still watching from the ledge, then started home.

18

His parents and Iku-lani welcomed him back with joy. Not so Kama-kahi. He summoned the other brothers and gave them orders. "Since we cannot rid ourselves of this troublesome sprout, we shall build a great canoe and set out for a new home, leaving him behind."

Kama-kahi called his kahuna—no one could build a seaworthy canoe without the ceremonies of a priest—and led the way to the upland forest where the tall koa trees grew. His nine brothers dutifully followed after.

Days passed and the brothers did not return. Aukele, remembering his grandmother's warning, went to the forest in search of them. Not wanting his brothers to know of his magic talismans, he hid his calabash in his secret place before leaving.

All day he searched and found not a trace of his brothers, heard not a stroke of a distant axe. As the sun began to set, he grew hungry and thought longingly of his life-giving leaf safely hidden at home. No use to wish for it now. Building a snare, he trapped two birds and made a fire to cook them. The appetizing aroma of roasting meat soon drifted upon the mountain air, setting Aukele's mouth to watering.

Aukele stooped to take the birds from the spit. Crashing through the woods came his brothers, Kama-kahi in the lead. "See this!" Kama-kahi cried. "Our young sprout has been preparing an evening meal for us! Very thoughtful!" He snatched the birds from the spit. Handing them to his brothers, he said, "Ah. All we need now is water and Aukele will fetch that for us. Back the way we came is a water hole with a big black rock at its entrance. Here! Fill this!"

What use to protest against ten? Aukele took the water gourd and went off. He found the water hole with the black rock at its entrance. In the fading light he saw crude steps leading down into a small cave where he could hear the sound of dripping water.

A twig snapped. Aukele whirled about, expecting to find Kama-kahi behind him, but the forest lay silent and desolate. The sun had set and the light was fading fast. He must hurry.

He made his way down the crude steps to the spring. The water trickling from the rock wall was cold and refreshing. Aukele drank his fill, then held the water gourd beneath the spring. As the water slowly neared the brim, something moved above him.

Looking up, he saw the malicious face of Kama-kahi, heard his gloating voice. "Drink deep, my upstart brother, for water is all that is left to you."

Kama-kahi's face disappeared. The rock was pushed into the opening above, shutting out the fading light, leaving Aukele a prisoner—once more in darkness, with only the sound of the trickling spring to break the lonely silence.

IKU-LANI

A Canoe Sails

Aukele had climbed the crude steps a half-dozen times, straining to raise the great rock at the top of the cave. The rock had not budged. He had stumbled about in the darkness, trying to find another way out. There was none. One thing he had not done—cry for help. What use? There was no one to hear but his brothers—and would Kama-kahi let them come to his aid? Not likely.

Aukele tried to keep account of the days by the bird-song he could hear above him each morning and each evening. One day passed . . . two . . . four . . . How long could a man remain alive on water alone? He was about to find out, he thought grimly. Six days . . . seven. . . . By the eighth day he was too weak to count. The song of the forest birds sounded fainter and fainter and he could no longer tell whether it was morning or evening.

Then suddenly, without warning, a shaft of light pierced the gloom. Looking up, Aukele saw the rock at the cave's entrance being rolled back. In the opening appeared the worried face of his young brother Iku-lani.

"O, my brother! Thanks be to Lono I found you in time!" Iku-lani cried.

"Barely . . ." Aukele whispered.

With Iku-lani's help, he managed to climb the steps, then collapsed on the rock above.

"I tried to come for you before this," Iku-lani explained, "but Kama-kahi kept all of us busy working on the canoe. Now it is finished. Tomorrow we sail."

"Tomorrow!" Aukele cried. "But I must go with you!"

"My brother, you cannot!" Iku-lani protested. "A long hard sea journey in your condition? It would be madness!"

"Help me home," Aukele said. "I have something from Great Mo-o Woman that will restore my strength."

"But, my brother—" Iku-lani hesitated, embarrassed.

"Yes?"

"Kama-kahi will never let you go with us! It is to get away from you that he plans this trip."

"I *must* go," Aukele insisted. "Unless I do, you will all die in a strange land. Die with neither kinsman nor friend to bury your bones."

Iku-lani smiled. "Have you forgotten what expert warriors Kama-kahi has made of us? Have no fear. We can defend ourselves."

"Not against sorcery," said Aukele. "Only I can do that."

Iku-lani considered this somberly. "There is one way we might manage it," he said. "Our nephew Sacred One. His father Kama-kahi can deny him nothing. Perhaps. . . . Be at the canoe-launching place at sunrise tomorrow. I will do my best."

22

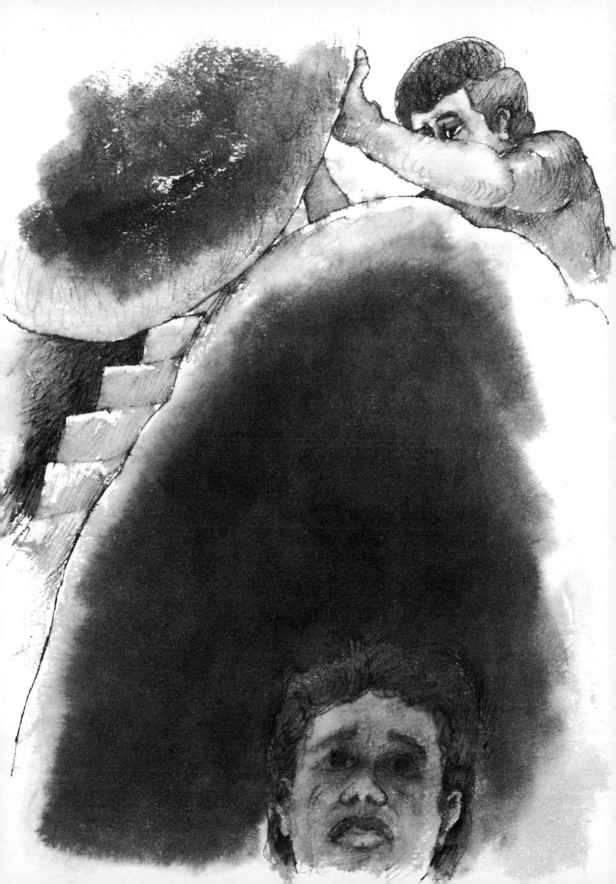

"My thanks, Iku-lani. Now if you will help me home—"

Aukele met further objections when he told his parents of his plan. "How can you consider such a thing?" his mother cried. "You know that Kama-kahi waits only for a chance to do away with you! Here, your father can protect you. Who will protect you among strangers? Your father will lose his favorite son!"

"If I do not go, my father will lose all ten sons," Aukele answered grimly. "Great Mo-o Woman has foretold it."

"What do you mean?" his father demanded.

"Grandmother has foreseen my brothers' deaths on this trip. I alone can save them—with her magic talismans."

His father turned to his wife. "No one could have stronger protection than that," he said at last. "We must let Aukele go."

At sunrise Aukele was at the launching place, his covered calabash in a netting slung about his neck.

Kama-kahi, overseeing the loading of the canoe, stopped short at sight of him. He looked as though he had seen a ghost. "You?" he cried.

"I have come to wish you well, my brother," said Aukele meekly.

"I can manage without your good wishes," Kama-kahi retorted sourly. "Stay out of the way!"

Aukele moved back, quietly watching as the loading proceeded. Soon Kama-kahi's son, Sacred One, went aboard and took his place on the pola. Iku-lani followed, carrying a great steering paddle. He gave Aukele a level glance but

24

passed on without a word. Aukele watched him place the oar on the canoe floor, then join Sacred One on the pola. The two talked together, glancing down to the spot where Aukele stood.

Then Sacred One came to the edge of the pola, waved, and called, "Aukele! Come aboard! I wish your company."

Kama-kahi turned with an angry "No!" But Sacred One, with a winning smile, said, "You will grant my wish, my father? It would be a lonesome journey for me without young company."

Scowling, his father nodded. Aukele scurried aboard before Kama-kahi could change his mind.

Disaster Threatens

THE SUN BEAT DOWN, burning the skin, parching the lips, making the eyeballs ache. Aukele squinted against the glare. As far as one could see there was nothing but endless ocean.

Four months of this—months in which strong winds filled their woven sails and blew them off-course. Months in which the winds died, leaving them drifting and lost. Months of straining at the paddles with no land in sight.

Now, food and water were nearly gone. The older brothers, racked by hunger and thirst, were sullen and irritable, their bodies gaunt, their eyes glazed. Only Aukele, Iku-lani, and Sacred One were strong and well-fed.

Kama-kahi, having conferred with the navigator with discouraging results, glared at Aukele. "You are the one who has brought the wrath of the gods upon us! Feed him to the sharks, my brothers! Then perhaps the gods will smile on us again."

KAMIKAHI

The two wrestling brothers sprang toward Aukele, eager to carry out the command.

"No!" The voice of Sacred One, young and high, rang out imperiously. "You must not, my father! Aukele alone can save us! He has a life-giving leaf. See how it has nourished the three of us."

Kami-kahi scowled, unbelieving. But the evidence was there before his eyes. His son and his two youngest brothers were strong and well-fed, while the rest were weak and emaciated.

Aukele spoke. "It is true, my brother. Taste and see." He took the life-giving leaf from his covered calabash and offered it to Kama-kahi.

Still sceptical, Kama-kahi raised it to his lips. All at once the color returned to his skin, the strength to his muscles. Soberly he passed the leaf to his navigator brother. From one to another the magic leaf made its way, until all were fed. Then Aukele returned it to his calabash. After that there was no more talk of tossing him overboard.

That same night, when Aukele lay down to sleep, the voice of Lono spoke to him softly from his calabash. Aukele listened respectfully to what his god had to say.

Next morning, Aukele made his announcement. "Good news, my brothers! Tomorrow at daybreak we sight the island of Holani-of-the-rising-sun. There we shall find food and water in abundance."

Kama-kahi turned questioningly to the sailing master. The man shrugged his shoulders. "I have no knowledge of this. We must wait and see."

That evening when darkness fell, the stone anchor was dropped over the side and there was sleep for all. As the sun rose, there, shimmering on the horizon, lay Holani-of-the-rising-sun. Upon reaching it, the voyagers found it to be small but beautiful indeed. Clean sandy beaches. Quiet sheltered coves. Tall green coconut palms and spreading breadfruit trees. Friendly people who showed them hidden springs of clear, cold water.

Four days and four nights the brothers and Sacred One remained on the island, enjoying the feel of land underfoot, the luxury of shade overhead.

Then Kama-kahi grew restless. "Time to be on our way!" he ordered.

"But why?" questioned one brother. "What can we find that is better than this?"

Kama-kahi snorted. "Do you wish to be champion of this overgrown rock? Out there are islands that offer a real challenge. When we find such a one, then we shall stay."

"Such an island lies to the west," said Aukele. "Holani-of-the-setting-sun. It holds the challenge you seek for it is ruled by the sorceress, Chiefess Namaka. All its people are her slaves. There lies your challenge—and death."

"Have you become a seer at such a tender age, Young Sprout?" Kama-kahi mocked. "If there is such a chiefess, I shall find and conquer her! Gather water and provisions! Tomorrow we sail on the morning breeze."

Again the burning sun, the blinding glare, the stormy winds and the endless calms. Again the failing food and water supply, the dependence upon Aukele's life-giving leaf. Then at last the voice of Lono speaking softly from the calabash—and, in the morning, Aukele's announcement.

"Today, when the sun sinks into the sea, we shall sight

Holani-of-the-setting-sun; an island with mountains to touch the stars."

Again Kama-kahi turned to the sailing master. Again the man shrugged. "He was right before, my brother."

Suddenly the wind died. The great double canoe began to drift aimlessly. Kama-kahi ordered all hands to the paddles. Throughout the day the brothers paddled and saw no sign of land. The sun moved slowly toward its

30

western portal and Kama-kahi's bitter voice challenged, "Well, Gifted Navigator?"

Aukele raised his arm. "There," he cried, pointing.

The clouds parted and they saw it—a beautiful green island with mountains to touch the stars.

"Now comes the time of danger," Aukele warned. "My brother, if you will put me in charge I can save us all."

Kama-kahi growled, "Are you then braver, stronger, more skillful than your champion brothers?"

Aukele shook his head impatiently. "It is not a matter of bravery, strength, or skill, my brother. This Chiefess Namaka is a sorceress with deadly powers. I alone have the means to deal with them."

"Enough!" roared Kama-kahi. "If you are so powerful, why did you not build your own canoe and set out to conquer this sorceress? I am in charge of this canoe and

in charge I shall remain!"

"Then one word of warning, my brother," said Aukele. "This chiefess will send out her four kupua brothers in bird form to greet you. Tell them you come in peace. Your life, your son's life, the lives of all your brothers, depend upon it."

Kama-kahi turned away scornfully.

As the canoe approached the island, four graceful birds —one white, one gray, one brown, one green—came flying to meet them. They circled overhead, then landed upon the pola.

The white bird spoke with a human voice. "What brings you to Holani-of-the-setting-sun?"

Kama-kahi gave Aukele a mocking glance, then answered, "Conquest!"

With a flapping of wings, the four birds flew off. Aukele gave a despairing cry.

Death Comes Stalking

AUKELE SNATCHED UP HIS calabash and moved to the pola's edge.

"Jump!" he cried to Iku-lani and Sacred One.

"Stay!" ordered Kama-kahi.

Aukele, knowing the boys would never disobey Kama-kahi, leaped into the sea and began swimming away from the canoe.

Looking toward shore, he saw a woman shaking a feather kahili. From it there came a blinding flash. Glancing over his shoulder, Aukele saw the canoe burst into a mass of flame and smoke.

By the time he had dragged himself ashore, the canoe, Aukele's ten brothers, his nephew—all had vanished beneath the waves.

"Not even in strange soil will my kinsmen's bones lie now, but on the ocean's floor," he mourned. With his calabash clutched tightly in his arms, Aukele fell into an

exhausted sleep. He woke to the barking of a dog in the distance and the sound of a voice nearby.

"Awake, Aukele! Death comes stalking!"

Aukele sat up and looked about. There was no one in sight. It was the voice of Lono, speaking from his calabash.

"O Lono, god of my family, tell me what to do," said Aukele.

Lono answered, "Chiefess Namaka sends her two kupua servants, Lizard Maiden and Rat Maiden, to kill you. Call them by name and win them to your side."

Soon two maidens appeared on the beach. One's head resembled a lizard's, the other a rat's. Aukele rose and went forward to meet them. "Greetings, Lizard Maiden. Greetings, Rat Maiden," he said.

A look of terror came over the two faces. This handsome stranger knew their names, knew their kupua power! He must be kupua too! And who knew how powerful he might be? Better to have him as friend than enemy.

"Welcome, stranger," Lizard Maiden said. "What brings you to Holani-of-the-setting-sun?"

"I come in peace," Aukele answered, "having heard of the beauty of your island from as far away as Land-supporting-the-heavens."

"Your canoe—where is it?" Rat Maiden asked.

"Auwe! Lost at sea and all my kinsmen with it!"

The two maidens exchanged glances. "Destroyed by our Chiefess Namaka," said Lizard Maiden, "and now she has sent us to destroy you!"

"And will you?" Aukele asked.

Lizard Maiden hesitated. "How can we destroy what we could not find? From beach to uplands we searched

LIZARD MAIDEN

and found no trace of a stranger."

Rat Maiden nodded. "The dog Moela barks at every scuttling crab. We saw no stranger."

"Mahalo. My warm thanks," said Aukele. The two left him.

Soon the voice of Lono sounded again. "Be on guard, Aukele. Death comes stalking once more."

"O Lono, god of my family, tell me what to do," Aukele cried.

The voice of Lono went on. "Chiefess Namaka sends her four kupua bird brothers to kill you. Call them by name and win them to your side."

Aukele turned around. From the hillside came four young men—tall, strong, good to look upon. Aukele went forward to meet them. Noting the color of each malo, he spoke.

"Greetings, White-bird-brother, Gray-bird-brother, Brown-bird-brother, Green-bird-brother," said Aukele.

Three of the men started toward him angrily, but White-

36

bird-brother held up a restraining hand.

"Greetings, stranger," he said. "Have you come to court death? Our sister, Death? Otherwise known as Chiefess Namaka?"

"To court and overcome her," Aukele replied.

White-bird-brother chuckled. "My brothers, this one could be her match! Think what it could mean to us!"

The three brothers considered the matter. "An end to interruptions of our konane games," said Gray-bird-brother.

"An end to preparing food for that noisy dog, Moela," mused Brown-bird-brother.

"An end to orders from a nagging woman!" said Green-bird-brother with feeling.

"Shall we take this stranger back with us?" White-bird-brother asked with a grin.

"Ae. Let us!" said the three in chorus.

White-bird-brother turned to Aukele. "She will set her dog on you. Can you protect yourself?"

"I can."

"Good. Then a word of warning. Do not enter Namaka's dwelling. Do not eat her food. Do not underestimate her. She is a powerful sorceress, this sister of ours."

"One moment." Aukele opened his calabash, took out his feather shoulder cape and put it on. Then, replacing the lid, he said, "I am ready."

Across the beach and up the hillside they went—White-bird-brother in the lead with Aukele at his side, the other brothers following.

They came to a dwelling where a feather kahili stood at the entrance. White-bird-brother called out, "We have found the one who set Moela barking, my sister."

"Bid him come in," came a voice from inside.

"I bid you come out," Aukele retorted.

"You bid me?" A woman's face appeared in the door-way. A woman such as Aukele had never seen before—handsome, tall, with back straight as a tree, hair long and glossy—and eyes blazing in anger.

"And who are you who bids me come out?" she demanded.

Aukele stepped forward and spoke.

"I am Aukele
From Land-supporting-the-heavens.
Aukele, favorite son of Iku and Kapapa;
Aukele, grandson of Chief-of-utter-darkness
And Great Mo-o Woman.
Aukele the traveler,
Aukele the fearless."

Namaka snatched the feather kahili from the ground and shook it. A sheet of flame flowed from it and enveloped Aukele. When it died, there he stood, unharmed. Great Mo-o Woman's fire cape had saved him.

Namaka glared. "Moela!" she called. A huge dog came bounding to her side. "Kill him!" she ordered.

The animal sprang at Aukele. Aukele whipped off his feather cape and shook it. In mid-leap, the dog dissolved into a heap of powdery ashes. Namaka stared, unbelieving. For a moment she was speechless, torn between rage at Aukele and sorrow at the loss of Moela.

"Is he not a rare find, my sister?" demanded White-bird-brother. "This one has courage and power to match your own!"

"Ae," said Namaka, but her eyes burned fiercely. "Let

38

us make him welcome." She clapped her hands. Servants came running with platters of food—such tempting food as Aukele had not seen in all those long days at sea. Roasted pig. Broiled fish. Baked yams. Pounded poi. His mouth watered at the appetizing aroma.

"My thanks, O Chiefess," he said. "I regret that I may eat only the food I have brought with me. A vow to my god." Lifting the lid of his calabash, he took out the life-giving leaf and held it to his lips.

Namaka stared in baffled silence. The four bird brothers gleefully watched this latest contest of wills.

RAT MAIDEN

Halulu-the-evil-one

THE SUN SHONE HIGH in the heavens. In the sleeping house of the bird brothers Aukele slept heavily.

In the meeting house Namaka held council with her brothers. "Who is this Aukele? What powerful magic does he possess?" she demanded. "He has escaped my fire kahili, reduced Moela to ashes, detected the poisoned food! He is too great a threat to us. You must kill him!"

"No," said White-bird-brother. "We will not."

Namaka's eyes blazed. "And why?"

"Because he is more valuable to us alive," one brother replied. "Think on it, my sister. In all the years you have ruled Holani-of-the-setting-sun has there ever appeared such a powerful one? And handsome as well. What do you gain by destroying such power? Why not add it to your own? Marry this Aukele! With him at your side you will be invincible!"

Slowly the anger left Namaka's face, to be replaced by

a crafty smile. "It could be that you are right," she conceded. "But before I consent to marry this stranger, he must meet Halulu-the-evil-one."

Gray-bird-brother protested. "You would send Aukele to meet that man-eating one? No one has ever escaped him!"

Namaka nodded. "Exactly. What better test could there be? If Aukele escapes Halulu I shall marry him."

All four brothers argued but Namaka remained stubborn.

When Aukele woke from his long sleep he washed, took nourishment from his life-giving leaf, and went in search of Chiefess Namaka.

She met him, smiling. "Aukele, those of equal power need not be adversaries," she said. "I am leaving for a day at the beach. Come join me."

Aukele accepted, taking his calabash with him. The day was clear and mild. Namaka chose a rocky spot where powerful waves broke upon the shore. Aukele eyed the water dubiously.

NAMAKA

"Afraid?" Namaka taunted. She ran and dove into the rough water. Aukele stopped to dig a hole in the sand for his calabash. Before he could cover it, the voice of Lono sounded in warning.

"Death comes flying, Aukele! Death from Halulu-the-evil one!"

Suddenly the sun was blotted out as a huge bird swooped down upon Aukele. He had barely time to snatch his calabash from the sand before he was grasped in the bird's cruel talons and carried aloft.

On and on the bird flew, to a deep and desolate valley. There he set Aukele down and flew off. Aukele looked about him. Three sides enclosed by sheer rock walls, the fourth by crashing surf. Escape from this place would not be easy. He whirled around at the sound of voices, then stared in disbelief. Men were crawling from caves in the rock walls—men such as Aukele had never seen before and hoped never to see again. Walking skeletons with thin, wasted bodies and dull, lifeless eyes. They stared at him mournfully.

"A fine meal for the Evil One!" croaked a thing of skin and bones.

"That fiendish bird will make no meal of me!" Aukele declared. "Tell me of this monster. When does he return?"

"At sunset . . . a strong wind . . . then Halulu comes. He carries off two of us at a time for his meal." The man spoke in little more than a whisper.

"Can't you hide in the caves?" Aukele asked.

"We do. He reaches in . . . sweeps us out."

"Cut off his wing with a sharp stone!"

"We tried. Cuts heal by magic. Only fire can destroy Halulu. We cannot make fire."

"I can," said Aukele. "Here is what we will do." Carefully he outlined his plan.

At sunset the men crawled into the deepest cave, as far inside as possible. Aukele, with his magic knife drawn, hid just inside the cave's mouth.

Soon a strong wind sprang up. There came the sound of rushing wings. A great shadow darkened the valley floor and Aukele saw the evil bird swoop down and fly toward the cave.

Into the cave's mouth came the right wing, groping . . . searching . . . hunting for its first victim. Aukele slashed

44

with his magic knife, severing the gigantic wing.

Halulu wheeled about with a scream of pain, then thrust his left wing into the cave. Aukele's magic knife severed it. One of the great claws reached in. Aukele chopped it off.

The cries of the bird were deafening now. Its other claw appeared and was severed like the first. With a wild shriek, the bird thrust its ugly head into the cave.

Aukele gave one powerful slash of the magic knife and the monstrous head toppled to the floor of the cave.

With cries of joy, the prisoners helped Aukele throw the remains of the evil bird onto the valley floor. Then Aukele, taking his fire cape from his calabash, swept it through the air. The body of Halulu-the-evil-one was consumed by fire. Only a great pile of bones and ashes remained.

All were free from the evil bird, but they were still prisoners in this valley fortress. "Let us now eat and sleep," Aukele advised. "Tomorrow we shall find a way to escape."

He shared his life-giving leaf with his fellow prisoners. Each man, for the first time since his arrival in this place, lay down to sleep in peace. To sleep in peace and wake to the sound of rushing wings. . . .

Sorceress Wife

"HALULU!" SOMEONE SCREAMED. "He's come back to life!"

The prisoners went scrambling into the farthest corners of the cave. But Aukele moved to the cave's opening and looked out. Looked out and saw two of the bird brothers coming toward him.

"E, Aukele!" called White-bird-brother. "Where are you?"

"Here!" Aukele answered joyfully. "Halulu is dead. Can you help us out of this valley?"

"We can," White-bird-brother replied. "See? Namaka sends a headless rainbow for you. Walk up its back." He pointed.

Aukele saw a half-rainbow forming. Its top rested on the pali, its bow curved down to the valley floor.

"Come forth! Come forth!" he called to the men inside the cave. "There is a way out!"

The men came stumbling from the cave, staring in won-

46

der at the two great birds that spoke in human voices.

"Lead the men up the rainbow path," White-bird-brother directed. "From the pali's top we will fly ahead and guide you home."

"Namaka will be overjoyed at your escape," said Gray-bird-brother. "From the moment she sent Halulu after you she regretted it."

"That's comforting to know," said Aukele wryly.

White-bird-brother nodded. "Our headstrong sister has developed a great love for you, although she will not admit it. If you would marry her, now is the time to take action."

Aukele led the prisoners to the rainbow's base. Gingerly he set foot upon its shimmering pathway. It supported him. Limping, hobbling, the others followed. Slowly, painfully, the procession made its way up the rainbow arch to the top of the pali. There, with warm thanks to Aukele and the bird brothers who had saved them from certain death, the men went their separate ways.

The bird brothers flew slowly and Aukele followed them on foot. As he went, he turned over in his mind the brothers' advice. Should he marry Namaka? There was little reason for him to return home. His ten brothers and young nephew were gone. No maiden waited for him in Land-supporting-the-heavens. Why not make his home on Holani-of-the-setting-sun? With his magic talismans he could protect himself from Namaka's sorcery, could see that she used her own powers mercifully. It would not be easy to have a powerful sorceress as wife, but his life would be a challenging one. What man wanted an easy life?

Namaka met him with tears of joy. Aukele was astonished. Was this the imperious chiefess with whom he had matched wits such a short time ago? She seemed more warm, less arrogant than he remembered her. If he wished to marry her, now was the time, as the brothers had advised. But it must be on his own terms.

Aukele spoke coldly. "Halulu is dead. I have come to hold you to your word."

Namaka—imperious Chiefess Namaka—actually blushed. Aukele observed her with astonishment. This woman was full of surprises.

So Aukele and Namaka were married. The first few days thereafter passed peacefully enough. Then Aukele made his first request. "I have need of new malo and sleeping kapa," he told Namaka. "It is time for you to begin kapa-making."

"I!" Namaka retorted. "Is kapa-making work for a chiefess?"

"No, it is work for a wife," Aukele answered, "and you are my wife as well as a chiefess. Come, I will help you gather the wauke bark."

"No!"

Aukele started toward her. With a stamp of her foot, Namaka vanished. In her place stood a tall gray stone.

Aukele picked it up easily, lifted it above his head. It changed in his hands to a dipperful of water. Undaunted, Aukele put the dipper to his lips. The dipper changed back to Namaka in her human form. Snatching up her feather kahili, she struck the ground with it. Flames billowed about Aukele, but his fire cape kept him from harm.

"Now," he said, "if the demonstration is over, let us gather wauke bark."

Namaka nodded meekly, but Aukele had a feeling that the battle was not yet over.

A little later, White-bird-brother asked, "Has our sister taught you how to fly, Aukele?"

Aukele, startled, answered, "She has not. Has she that power also?"

"She has indeed," said Gray-bird-brother.

"We could teach you secretly," White-bird-brother suggested mischievously. "No need for her to know until the matter is done."

"Teach me!" said Aukele with a grin.

Flying Lessons

INSIDE THE MEN'S EATING house the flying lesson was underway, with the four bird brothers gathered about their pupil.

"Leap up to that shelf and hold on!" White-bird-brother ordered.

Aukele leaped up and held on.

"A good start," said Gray-bird-brother. "Now leap to the rafters and hold on."

Aukele hesitated, then made a wild leap. His fingers caught at a rafter, caught and slipped. Down he came with a thud.

"That will bring Namaka running," said White-bird-brother. "Quickly! Box with me!"

Outside they heard running footsteps. The voice of Namaka called out, "My husband, what was that noise?"

Aukele poked his head through the doorway. "Your brothers are teaching me to box," he said. "And auwe!

50

What formidable teachers!"

"Oh. Take care," said Namaka, and went back to the women's eating house.

"Now, try again," said Gray-bird-brother. "The rafters. This time, hold fast."

Aukele leaped again, caught the rafter, and clung there. His face grew red with the strain of holding on.

"Maikai! Good! Now, let go. Wave your arms as you drop," Gray-bird-brother directed.

So glad was Aukele to ease his aching muscles that he forgot to wave his arms. Down he came with a crash.

"Auwe! That will bring Namaka again!" cried Green-bird-brother. "Quickly! Wrestle with me!"

Again the sound of running footsteps. Again the voice of Namaka calling out, "And that noise, my husband?"

Again Aukele poked his head through the doorway. "Now your brothers are teaching me to wrestle," he said. "And auwe! It is a hard lesson!" Grimacing, he rubbed his hip.

"Take care, my husband," said Namaka, and went off.

"Let us practice outdoors, behind the house," Brown-bird-brother suggested. They moved outside.

"Climb up on the roof," said Brown-bird-brother.

Aukele climbed to the thatched roof and stood there, looking down dubiously.

"Jump! And wave your arms!"

Aukele took a deep breath, jumped, and waved his arms. This time he sailed down and landed with only a slight jar.

"Better. Much better," said Green-bird-brother. "Now, take off from the ground."

On and on went the practice. Before long Aukele was

soaring over the housetop, swooping in graceful circles, thoroughly enjoying the novel sensation of flight.

The bird brothers watched with approval, then with some concern, as Aukele flew farther and farther. Flew until he became a mere speck in the evening sky.

Aukele was having a fine time. He startled a flock of seabirds, flew with them for a distance, then landed in a treetop. After a brief rest, he took off again in the direction he had come. When he saw below him the rooftops and the watching bird brothers, he dipped his wings in greeting, flew past, and circled back. Gliding down, he landed lightly on the rooftop below and looked down for his instructors' approval. Looked down and saw, not the admiring faces of the bird brothers, but the angry face of Namaka. Auwe! He had landed on the wrong roof!

For days Namaka went about in a rage. Angry with her brothers for having taught Aukele to fly, angry with Aukele for having learned the one magic power that had given her an advantage over him. But as time went by and Aukele showed no sign of using his flying ability to defy or desert her, Namaka was reassured.

One day, when the family was gathered together, she said, "My brothers, now that Aukele can fly, it is time that he met some of our kinfolk. Fly with him into the far heavens and present him to our uncle. Explain that Aukele is now my husband, that I share with him all my possessions—the things above and the things below, the things in the uplands and the things in the lowlands, the great things and the small things."

Aukele and the brothers were eager to set out. They left on a clear sunny morning, and Aukele, wearing his feather

cape, soared with the bird brothers, enjoying the warmth of the sun, the cooling breeze, the freedom of flight. Faster and faster he flew. So fast that he soon left the bird brothers behind. So fast that he did not hear their warning cries.

The sky grew darker but Aukele paid little attention. On and on he flew, until a rumble of thunder shook the heavens. On and on, until he saw, standing astride a dark cloud bank, the wrathful figure of a god with a thunderbolt aimed directly at his head.

An Announcement
and a Quest

A CLAP OF THUNDER WENT reverberating through the heavens, leaving Aukele rocking in its wake.

"Wait! I come from Namaka!" he cried. But his words were drowned out by the thunderous echoes.

The god, seeing him unharmed, hurled a spear of lightning that seemed to pierce Aukele's very bones. Only his fire cape saved him from disaster.

Before the god could loose another spear, Aukele heard shouts behind him. "Take refuge within a cloud!" White-bird-brother cried.

"No need for that," Aukele retored. "I shall kill this noisy fellow and save us all." He reached up to remove his fire cape.

"No! Wait!" cried White-bird-brother. "The god is your wife's uncle! Let me speak to him!"

At sight of White-bird-brother, Thunder God lowered his lightning spear. "What of Namaka?" he demanded.

"Has this young wizard done away with her? How else would he get up here?"

White-bird-brother held up a restraining hand. "Namaka is well, my uncle. This is her husband, Aukele. She sent us to tell you that she now shares with him all her possessions: 'the things above and the things below, the things in the uplands and the things in the lowlands, the great things and the small things.'"

Thunder God gave a sheepish grin. "My apologies, Aukele. You should have identified yourself."

"I tried," Aukele said ruefully. "But you have a powerful voice, my uncle!"

The other brothers joined the group. Soon the kinsmen were chatting together. Great rumbles of mirth shook the heavens when Thunder God heard of Aukele's flying lessons and the landing on Namaka's roof.

"I've not had such an enjoyable time in many moons," Thunder God said after awhile, wiping his streaming eyes. "I am sorry to see you go. Come again soon."

When the five reached home, Namaka welcomed them warmly. She listened with amusement to the tale of Aukele's encounter with Thunder God. "It is clear that you are well able to defend yourself, even against the gods. I too have some news, my husband. We are to have a child."

Aukele received the news with gladness. "A son, of course!" he ordered.

"Of course," Namaka answered, smiling.

But as the days went by, Namaka noticed a growing sadness in Aukele. "You are not happy about our coming child, my husband?" she asked.

"I am, truly," Aukele answered. "But thoughts of a child

remind me of my brother Iku and my young nephew, lost at sea when you destroyed their canoe. How can I be happy with a wife and son while they wander in the land of lost souls?"

Namaka brooded on the matter, torn between remorse and fear; remorse at what she had done, fear at what she must do. Reluctantly she spoke.

"There is a way they might be restored, my husband. A way most dangerous—"

"No matter! Tell me!"

"If you could fetch some of the Water of Life, I could restore them."

"Where do I find this water?" Aukele asked eagerly.

"It is kept closely guarded in the Cavern of Night where the sun goes each evening to rest. You must fly in a straight course toward the setting sun, veering neither to left nor to right, lest you be lost and wander endlessly through the heavens."

"Fly a straight course toward the setting sun," Aukele repeated carefully. "It does not sound dangerous."

"Ah, but that is only the beginning. Once in the Cavern of Night, you must pass four fearsome guardians, then Ka-moho-alii himself, keeper of the Water of Life. Should you manage to escape him, there will still be the four guardians waiting for your return. It is a most hazardous undertaking, my husband. I wish you would not go," Namaka finished mournfully.

"I must," said Aukele.

Perilous Flight

As the sun sank into the western sea, Aukele set a straight course and flew toward it. On . . . and on . . . and on. Never had he attempted such a long flight. His arms grew weary, the calabash in its sling bumped against his chest. He longed to stop and rest but, flying over the sea, there was no place to perch, even for a moment.

He flew slower . . . and slower. Somehow he seemed to be no nearer his goal than when he had set out. His eyes closed wearily.

"Aukele! Death comes flying!" The voice of Lono shocked him into wakefulness. Dismayed, Aukele saw that the sun had already set, not directly ahead of him but far to his right. "You have left the straight course," Lono continued. "We are lost—and trouble lies ahead!"

Trouble indeed, and it was not long in coming. Suddenly the sun was blotted out by a black cloud that drenched Aukele with icy rain and set his teeth to chattering. But

59

the rain soon passed and Aukele saw beyond it a glimmering rainbow. Remembering his climb out of the valley on another such bow, he flew to it and set foot upon it. But auwe! This rainbow vanished swiftly and Aukele felt himself falling headlong through space.

"Fly up! Fly up!" cried Lono. Making a great effort, Aukele flew up. Up into a thick, smothering bank of fog. He groped his way through it, came out, shivering, beyond it. Came out to see before him another dark cloud, and on it, a thunderbolt in each great fist, the fierce but familiar figure of Thunder God.

"Thunder God! Save me! It is your nephew who calls!"

Aukele's plea was lost in the vast rumble as Thunder God swept past him, unseeing, unhearing. As the thundercloud moved on, Aukele saw the first faint star of evening.

"Fly up and take hold of the star!" Lono cried.

Aukele, chilled to the bone, achingly weary, flew up. But before he could grasp the star, it shot past him through the evening sky, trailing a tail of fire behind it.

"We are lost," Aukele cried in despair. "I can fly no farther."

"Not so," replied Lono. "The moon is rising. Fly to it and hold fast!"

Aukele looked and saw a quarter moon rising. With one last desperate effort he flew to it, caught hold of its lower tip, and hung there, exhausted.

Moon God glared at him. "Who are you that dares to touch Moon God?" he demanded. "Even my granddaughter, Namaka, has never done that!"

Gasping for breath, Aukele tried to identify himself.

60

"I am Aukele

From Land-supporting-the-heavens.

Aukele, favorite son of—"

He could go no farther.

Moon God reached down to toss him into space. Aukele found strength enough for one despairing cry. "Aukele . . . husband of your granddaughter, Namaka!"

"You lie!" roared Moon God. "Namaka's husband is dead! All her kinfolk in the heavens have just been summoned to mourn his passing. Had I not overslept I should be down there now. You are an imposter!"

"Not so!" Aukele protested. "I have lost my way and been gone a long time. Namaka must have thought me dead."

"How can I believe you?" demanded Moon God.

"My god Lono will tell you."

From Aukele's calabash came the voice of his god.

"This is Aukele

From Land-supporting-the-heavens.

Aukele, favorite son of Iku and Kapapa,

Aukele, grandson of Chief-of-utter-darkness

And Great Mo-o Woman.

Aukele the traveler,

Aukele the fearless,

Aukele, husband of Chiefess Namaka."

"I believe," said Moon God. He gave a vast chuckle of mirth. "Wait until Namaka sees this! Her grandfather, come tardily to mourn her dead husband, and bringing with him that husband, alive and well!"

Cavern of Night

As AUKELE NEARED HOME with Moon God, sounds of mourning reached them from the Long House.

"Let me go first," said Moon God. He stepped through the doorway. Aukele, waiting outside, saw Namaka come to greet him with tear-stained face. But sorrow had not dimmed her spirit.

"How late you are, my grandfather!" she said. "Is my mourning so unimportant to you?"

Moon God shook his head. "Not unimportant, Namaka— unnecessary."

Namaka's eyes flashed with anger. "Unnecessary? I have lost my beloved husband, Aukele!"

"You have lost him temporarily," Moon God corrected, "and your grandfather has found him." He turned to the doorway and beckoned. Aukele entered.

Namaka ran to him with a joyful cry. "My husband! Alive and well! Behold, all my kinfolk have come from the heavens to mourn your passing!"

Aukele gave a wry grin. "Well I know! Their passing was nearly the death of me!"

Mourning turned to merriment. God and goddess of sun, rain, and rainbow, of fog, thunder, lightning, and stars, celebrated Aukele's return, while Moon God looked on benevolently.

Presently Namaka's kinsmen returned to their duties in the heavens and life for Aukele and Namaka went on as before. But the cheerful gathering of relatives had revived Aukele's sorrow for his own lost family. There came a day when Aukele knew that he must set out again in search of the Water of Life—find it or have no rest. Namaka pleaded with him not to go, but Aukele insisted. "This time will be less hazardous," he argued. "I know the way. I know the dangers to avoid."

So once more, with his feathered cape about his shoulders, his netted calabash about his neck, Aukele set out in search of the Water of Life.

This time he found the Cavern of Night with little difficulty, entered the dark tunnel, and climbed down to the rocky floor. Blinded by the rays of the setting sun hurrying along the passage before him, he did not see the shadowy figure barring his way until he was upon him. A fiercely scowling warrior, wearing black malo and black crested helmet, stood before him, holding a black-topped kapu stick. He struck the rocky floor with it, once . . . twice . . . three times . . . and four. Then, raising the kapu stick menacingly, he cried out:

"Kapu! Kapu!
The Cavern of Night is kapu!
Who comes? Who comes?"

Aukele took a deep breath and, in a voice as strong as

he could make it, gave answer:

"I, Aukele, come
From Land-supporting-the-heavens.
Aukele, favorite son of Iku—"

He got no farther.

The fierce scowl of the warrior guard gave way to a delighted grin. "You are Aukele, son of my nephew Iku? Greetings, Aukele! What brings you to Cavern of Night?"

"I come for the Water of Life to restore my ten brothers and my nephew lost at sea," Aukele answered.

First Guard nodded. "A worthy cause but a dangerous one, Aukele. The way is filled with traps. However, I will do what I can to help a kinsman. When you come to the grove of loulu palms, keep to the left. They are planted so close together that if you touch a single frond it will set the rest to clattering and warn Ka-moho-alii. The ears that one has! He can hear an ant tramping on a blade of grass! Go softly, Aukele, and watch for Second Guard."

Aukele thanked First Guard and went on his way. On to the grove of loulu palms, keeping to the left and touching not a single frond. On—until his way was blocked by Second Guard. He too wore black malo and black crested helmet, and in his hand he held a wicked spear. He struck the rocky floor with it, once . . . twice . . . three times . . . and four. Then, raising the spear menacingly, he cried out:

"Kapu! Kapu!
The Cavern of Night is kapu!
Who comes? Who Comes?"

Aukele made answer:

"I, Aukele, come,
From Land-supporting-the-heavens.
Aukele, favorite son of Iku and Kapapa—"

He got no farther.

Second Guard's spear went clattering to the ground and Aukele was crushed in his great arms.

"You are Aukele, son of my niece Kapapa? Greetings, Aukele! What brings you to Cavern of Night?"

Aukele explained his mission. Second Guard nodded. "I will do what I can to help a kinsman," he said. "Soon you will come to a grove of bamboo. Keep to the right, for if you once enter it, you will find yourself in a maze which will hold you prisoner for Ka-moho-alii. The eyes that one has! He can see a flea jumping upon a dog's back. Go slowly, Aukele, and watch for Third Guard."

Aukele thanked Second Guard and went on his way. On to the bamboo grove, keeping to the right and avoiding the maze. On until his way was blocked by Third Guard. He, like the others, wore black malo and crested helmet. He was older than the other two, but his hands, holding a monstrous club, were strong and muscular. He struck the rocky floor with his club, once . . . twice . . . three times . . . and four. Then raising the club menacingly, he cried out:

> "Kapu! Kapu!
> The Cavern of Night is kapu!
> Who comes? Who comes?"

Aukele made answer:

> "I, Aukele, come,
> From Land-supporting-the-heavens.
> Aukele, favorite son of Iku and Kapapa—"

That was as far as he got.

Third Guard's club went crashing to the ground and Aukele was squeezed in his muscular arms.

"You are Aukele, son of my daughter Kapapa? Greetings, Aukele! What brings you to Cavern of Night?"

Aukele explained. Third Guard nodded and said, "I will do what I can to help a kinsman. Soon you will come to a grove of lama trees. Keep to the narrow center path, for the fruit of those trees is poisonous. If a single one falls on you, you will die! And nothing would please Ka-moho-alii more! Go warily, Aukele, and watch for Fourth Guard."

Aukele thanked Third Guard and went on his way. On to the grove of lama trees, keeping to the narrow center path and avoiding the poisonous fruit. On, until he found his way going steeply down and out onto an open plain, with the sound of the sea in the distance.

In the dim light he stumbled over a huddled figure. It was an aged woman, wearing black pa-u and black feather headband. She sat at a kapa board with a bowl of black dye before her, and in her hand she held a heavy wooden kapa beater. She struck her kapa board with it, once . . . twice . . . three times, and four. Then, raising the beater menacingly, she cried out:

"Kapu! Kapu!
The Cavern of Night is kapu!
Who comes? Who comes?"

Aukele made answer:
"I, Aukele, come,
From Land-supporting-the-heavens.
Aukele, favorite son of Iku and Kapapa;
Aukele, grandson of Chief-of-utter-darkness
And Great Mo-o Woman—"

That was as far as he got.

The woman threw down her kapa beater and rose to

her feet. She stretched out her hands, running her fingers lightly over his face, and Aukele realized that she was sightless. Tears ran down her cheeks as she spoke. "You are Aukele, grandson of my sister Great Mo-o Woman? Greetings, Aukele! What brings you to Cavern of Night?"

As Aukele explained, she nodded her head. "I, Woman-who-walks-in-darkness, will do what I can to help a kinsman. But it is no easy task you have set for yourself, Aukele. Ka-moho-alii himself still guards the Water of Life. He will recognize you as an intruder, on sight, for we who dwell in Cavern of Night are dark-skinned and dress in black. If you are to escape detection you must look like us."

"But how?" Aukele questioned.

Woman-who-walks-in-darkness took a garment from her pile of kapa. "Here is one of the black malo I make for the men who dwell here. Go put it on. Then we will darken your skin."

Aukele did as she bid him. When he returned, she daubed his face and neck with dye, then handed him the bowl. "Now your hands and arms, your feet and legs," she directed.

When the disguise was complete the sightless woman gave further instructions. "You must go straight ahead until you come to the gleaming white stone that covers Ka-moho's pit. Lift it and reach your hand down. Do not speak, for your voice will betray you. If you are lucky, Ka-moho's servants will mistake you for him and hand you the gourd containing the Water of Life. If they do, take it and run fast, before Ka-moho discovers you! The temper that one has! He would chop off your head first, then ask whose it was later!"

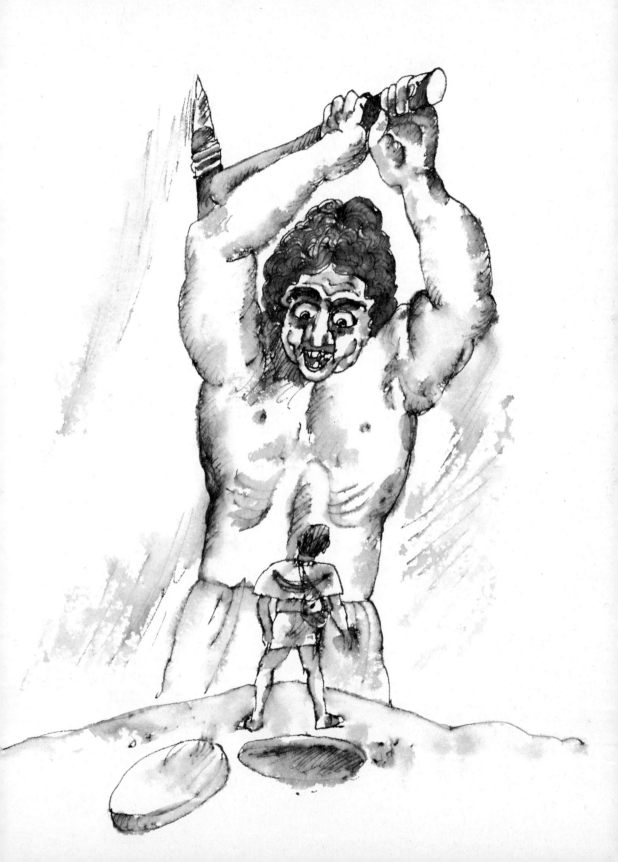

Aukele thanked Woman-who-walks-in-darkness and hurried on. On to the gleaming white stone, which he lifted and set aside. Kneeling at the rim of the pit below, he took a deep breath and reached down.

From below he heard a puzzled voice exclaim, "Ka-moho-alii is early! Bring meat! Quickly!"

Soon a bundle of roasted meat was placed in his hand. Aukele shrugged, ate the meat, and reached down again.

"He is still hungry! Bring fish!"

A packet of broiled fish was placed in his hand. Aukele grinned, ate the fish, and reached down once more.

"He is thirsty! Bring the Water of Life!"

A netted gourd with a stopper was placed in his hands. Aukele shook it, heard it gurgle, and got to his feet. Turning, he saw, towering above him, the monstrous figure of Ka-moho-alii. He caught a glimpse of white teeth gleaming in an evil grin, a flashing axe blade descending toward him.

Reunion

AUKELE DARTED BETWEEN KA-MOHO'S legs, heard the great axe land with a thud where his head had been but a second before, and ran as fast as his own legs would carry him.

Across the plain, past the house of Woman-who-walks-in-darkness, he ran. "Stop him!" cried the voice of Ka-moho, but the woman did not seem to hear. Up the steep path and back into the tunnel Aukele ran, until he reached the grove of lama trees. Along the narrow center path between the poison-fruited trees he ran, Ka-moho close behind him.

"Stop him!" shouted Ka-moho again. Third Guard came at Aukele with his monstrous club but somehow he missed him. With a cry of rage, Ka-moho swung his gleaming axe at one of the trees. Down came a shower of poison fruit, striking Aukele's head, his shoulders, his back. A blinding pain shot through him and he felt himself grow weak.

Dimly he heard the voice of Lono saying, "Aukele! The Water of Life! Take a sip!"

Still running, Aukele pulled the stopper and set the gourd to his lips, letting a few drops run down his throat. At once his pain vanished and his strength returned. Plunging the stopper back in place, he ran on. On to the bamboo grove, keeping to the left to avoid the treacherous maze through which he had come.

"Stop him!" yelled Ka-moho for the third time. Second Guard thrust forth his great spear, yet failed to strike him. In a fury, Ka-moho again swung his gleaming axe. Aukele dodged. Dodged—and found himself in the bamboo maze. Left . . . right . . . forward . . . back! No matter which way he ran he found himself at a dead end, with Ka-moho coming ever closer. Faintly he heard the voice of Lono saying, "Aukele! Your magic knife! Cut your way through!"

Still running, Aukele drew out his magic knife, cut his way through the bamboo maze, and pressed on. On to the loulu grove, keeping to the right to avoid the palm fronds.

"Stop him!" bellowed Ka-moho. Third Guard came at him, wielding his kapu stick, but his aim was poor and the stick glanced off. With a howl of frustration, Ka-moho swung his gleaming axe once more.

Aukele had but one choice—if he did not wish to part with his head! Swiftly he dodged into the loulu grove. Dodged Ka-moho's axe—and found that the loulu palms were set so closely together that he could not squeeze between them. They held him captive.

Grinning, Ka-moho strode toward him.

With almost his last breath Aukele whispered, "Lono! What shall I do now?"

72

"Your fire cape! Destroy the palms!" Lono ordered.

Aukele snatched off his cape and whirled it. There came a flash of flame, a cloud of smoke. When the smoke cleared, nothing remained of the loulu grove but a drift of ashes. And coming through those ashes—Ka-moho!

On ran Aukele. On ran Ka-moho. In the distance Aukele could see daylight from the mouth of the tunnel. But Ka-moho was gaining fast.

Aukele made a last desperate spurt. He was on the steep path leading up to the cavern's mouth when he tripped and fell. Ka-moho gave a wild yell and leaped for him.

This time, Aukele did not wait to ask his god for guidance. He scrambled to his feet, flapped his arms, and flew. Up . . . up . . . up . . . out of the darkness . . . out of the Cavern of Night . . . into the dazzling sunrise.

Ka-moho, blinded by the light, uttered a baffled roar and retreated. Aukele flew on . . . away from the Cavern of Night . . . over the ocean . . . toward home.

When he reached the region where the canoe had disappeared, Aukele drew the stopper from the gourd and spilled out the Water of Life.

Hovering over the spot, he waited. Nothing happened. No canoe appeared . . . no brothers . . . no nephew. Only a distant cry, carried by the offshore breeze.

"Aukele! No!" It was Namaka, crying out as she flew to meet him. "Only I can restore your kinfolk! Is the Water of Life all gone, Aukele?"

Aukele shook the gourd. Shook it and heard only a faint gurgle. "A little remains," he said sadly.

"Pour it into my hands," commanded Namaka, cupping her palms. Aukele did so. She sprinkled the water on the

73

sea below and spoke sternly. "Fly home without looking back!"

Reluctantly, Aukele started home. Was the Water of Life working? Had there been too little left to be effective? Some giant force seemed to be pulling at him, trying to turn his head—the temptation to look back was nearly unbearable. "Lono, give me strength," Aukele murmured.

He stared straight ahead and saw the four bird brothers flying to meet him with welcoming cries. Saw Rat Maiden and Lizard Maiden waving to him from the beach. Saw the men's eating house where he had learned to fly, Namaka's house where he had landed on the roof. Then, at last, the

dwelling where he and Namaka made their home. Down he flew, Namaka close behind him.

"Now you may look back," she said in his ear.

Aukele looked out to sea. Looked and saw the great canoe of Kama-kahi heading shoreward, sails billowing in the breeze, Iku-lani and Sacred One waving from the pola.

Aukele turned to Namaka with a joyous smile. "Thank you, Namaka! But wait!" He took the gourd from her. "Hold out your hands."

Puzzled, Namaka did as he bid. Four slow drops fell into her palm. She looked at her husband questioningly.

"I know you have missed Moela," Aukele said.

Smiling, Namaka sprinkled the drops upon the ground where Aukele had turned her dog to ashes. There came a happy bark and Moela was at Namaka's side once more.

The three, Aukele, Namaka, and Moela—man, wife, and guardian dog—moved to the beach to greet Aukele's kinsmen.

MOELA

Bibliography

Beckwith, Martha W. *Hawaiian Mythology*. New Haven: Yale University Press, 1940.

Fornander, Abraham. *Collection of Hawaiian Antiquities and Folklore*. 3 vols. Honolulu: Bishop Museum Press, 1916-1919.

Westervelt, William D. *Hawaiian Legends of Ghosts and Ghost-Gods*. Rutland, Vermont: Charles E. Tuttle Co., 1963.

Characters

Aukele (A-u-*ke*-le): youngest son of High Chief Iku

Bird Brothers: Chiefess Namaka's kupua brothers able to appear as bird or man

    Brown-bird-brother
    Gray-bird-brother
    Green-bird-brother
    White-bird-brother

Chief-of-utter-darkness: husband of Great Mo-o Woman; Aukele's grandfather

Guards: protectors of Water of Life in Cavern of Night

    First Guard
    Second Guard
    Third Guard
    Fourth Guard (Woman-who-walks-in-darkness)

Great Mo-o Woman: Aukele's grandmother

Halulu (Ha-*lu*-lu): the-evil-one; Namaka's man-eating bird

Iku (*I*-ku): High Chief of Land-supporting-the-heavens

Iku-lani (*I*-ku-*la*-ni): Aukele's youngest brother; the only kind one

Kama-kahi (*Ka*-ma-*ka*-hi): Aukele's eldest brother; a cruel tyrant who hates Aukele

Ka-moho-alii (Ka-*mo*-ho-a-*li*-i): keeper of Water of Life

Kapapa (Ka-*pa*-pa): mother of Aukele

Lizard Maiden: one of Chiefess Namaka's kupua servants

Lono: Aukele's family god

Moela (Mo-*e*-la): Chiefess Namaka's guardian dog

Moon God: Chiefess Namaka's grandfather

Namaka (Na-*ma*-ka): chiefess ruler of Holani-of-the-setting-sun; a sorceress; becomes Aukele's wife

Rat Maiden: one of Chiefess Namaka's kupua servants

Sacred One: Kama-kahi's cherished son

Thunder God: Chiefess Namaka's uncle

Woman-who-walks-in-darkness: blind Fourth Guard of Water of Life

Glossary

The Hawaiian language uses only twelve English letters: five vowels (a-e-i-o-u) and seven consonants (h-k-l-m-n-p-w).

The vowels usually sound like this:

a - like a in *far*   i like ee in *see*
e - like e in *bet*   o - like o in *sole*
u - like oo in *moon*

The consonants are sounded as in English except that w, in some positions, has the sound of v.

These rules will help you with pronunciation:

Every syllable ends with a vowel. (ka-hi-li)

Every vowel is sounded. (Ka-mo-ho-a-li-i)

Accented syllables are shown in italics.

ae (*a*-e), yes

aumakua (*a*-u-ma-*ku*-a), a family god or guardian spirit

auwe! (a-u-*we*), alas! Oh no!

e, a hail or greeting

Holani (Ho-*la*-ni), a far island
   of-the-rising-sun
   of-the-setting-sun

kahili (ka-*hi*-li), a feather standard, symbol of royalty
   Chiefess Namaka's kahili had the power to cause fire

kahuna (ka-*hu*-na), a priest or advisor

kapa (*ka*-pa), cloth made from bark of the wauke shrub

kapu (*ka*-pu), forbidden; kapu stick, a symbol of authority

Kauai (Ka-u-*a*-i), one of Hawaiian islands

konane (ko-*na*-ne), a game played with pebbles

kupua (ku-*pu*-a), supernatural; able to change form

lama (*la*-ma), a tree with poisonous fruit

loulu (*lo*-u-lu), a type of palm

mahalo (ma-*ha*-lo), thank you

maikai (ma-i-*ka*-i), good

malo (*ma*-lo), loincloth

Maui (*Ma*-u-i), one of Hawaiian islands

Oahu (O-*a*-hu), one of Hawaiian islands

pali (*pa*-li), a cliff

pa-u (*pa*-*u*), woman's skirt

pola (*po*-la), a platform on a large double canoe

wauke (*wa*-u-ke), shrub whose bark is used in making kapa

VIVIAN L. THOMPSON has written several distinguished books based on Hawaiian folklore, among them *Maui-Full-of-Tricks*, published by Golden Gate in 1970, *Hawaiian Myths of Earth, Sea and Sky*, and *Hawaiian Legends of Tricksters and Riddlers* (Holiday House). Many years' residency in the Islands and an ever-growing interest in things Polynesian led her to explore Hawaii's rich cultural heritage and to recreate its folk tales for today's readers. Born in New Jersey and educated there and in New York, Mrs. Thompson first came to Hawaii in 1949. Since then she has lived with her husband, an automotive engineer, on a sugar plantation at the foot of Mauna Kea on the island of Hawaii. In addition to her Hawaiian tales, she has written a number of books for young children.

EARL THOLLANDER is a painter and an illustrator who has a special fondness for things Hawaiian. He has made several drawing trips to the Islands and, like Vivian Thompson, has a keen interest in Hawaii's folklore. He has illustrated many books for a young audience, including Mrs. Thompson's *Maui-Full-Of Tricks* and *Keola's Hawaiian Donkey* (Golden Gate). He makes his home in Northern California near the little town of Calistoga.